Chocolate Chuckles

PAM HARVEY

Illustrated by Janine Dawson

sundance™

A Haights Cross Communications Company

The Story Characters

Sally

Mom

Grandpa & Grandma

The Story Setting

Sally's Place

Park

To Grandma
and Grandpa's

TABLE OF CONTENTS

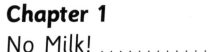

CHAPTER 1

No Milk!

"There's no milk!" said Mom. She turned around and glared at me.

I didn't say a word.

Luckily for me, the kitchen was full of chips, cheese and crackers, pickled onions, streamers, and party hats. In the middle of it all was a huge birthday cake. "Happy 80th Birthday" was written on it.

7

Lucky for me because Mom couldn't
see the empty milk carton I'd just been
drinking from.

"He'll want a cup of tea. And he won't drink it without milk," said Mom.

He was Grandpa, the birthday boy, who drank 20 cups of tea a day. He used the same tea bag all day. He lugged it around in a little green tin in his pocket. Disgusting!

"I have to go out and get some more milk." Mom looked at me sternly. "You stay here, Sally, in case Grandpa and Grandma arrive early. And don't touch anything. Promise?"

Me? Touch anything? Sometimes Mom sounds like she just doesn't trust me. I nodded very seriously, though, so she could go to the store without worrying.

"Fifteen minutes. That's all I'll be,"
said Mom. She picked up the car keys
and ran out the door.

I sat at the kitchen table. The smells of lemon frosting, cake, cheese, and chips drifted around me. But I didn't touch anything.

Except one cupcake and one potato chip—but they didn't really count.

Something was bugging me, and I had to nibble to help me think. Something was missing from the party food, and I didn't mean the cupcake and the potato chip. It was something very important.

Then it came to me—there were no
chocolate crackles!

What's a party without chocolate
crackles? Things were desperate. I had
to try to make some—fast. Mom
would be back in less than 13
minutes. I rushed into the kitchen.

CHAPTER 2

Making Chocolate Crackles

I bolted across to the pantry and pulled open the door.

Have you ever made chocolate crackles?
Well, I hadn't. But I'd eaten one
million seven hundred and sixty-five
thousand in my lifetime. So you'd
think I'd know what was in them.

I thought very hard. Mom had made
chocolate crackles for every one of my
birthdays. I could picture her mixing
bowl in my head. Hmmm.

In it there was puffed rice cereal, chocolate, and some white stuff. And there was some sort of cooking glue to hold it all together.

The Rice Puffs were in a see-through, plastic container. I poured a heap into the bowl. Cocoa could be the chocolate stuff. But the white stuff was a little harder to find.

Have you ever noticed pantries are full of white stuff? Containers filled with stuff that looks like baby powder.

My best guess for the mystery white stuff was sugar. But I ate some, and it was too gritty. Chocolate crackles don't feel gritty when you chomp into them. I knew the white stuff couldn't be flour because then they wouldn't be chocolate crackles. They'd be chocolate cakes.

Finally, I found some white stuff that wasn't gritty or floury. The label said it was baking soda. That could be it.

I poured the whole box into the bowl. Then, to hold it all together, I dumped in some olive oil.

Mix, mix, mix.

It looked perfect: brown, gooey, and bubbly. It was just a matter of dropping lumps of batter into cupcake papers and BINGO! Chocolate crackles.

CHAPTER 3

The Party

I put a plate of chocolate crackles on the table with the party food.

Just then, I heard Mom pull up in the driveway. Another car pulled up right behind her. So I had time to wash the mixing bowl.

Chocolate crackle batter was stuck to my fingers, so I licked it off.

There was something strange about the taste. I figured that was because the batter wasn't set.

The taste grew stronger in my mouth. It was really odd. I downed a glass of water. Just then Grandpa, Grandma, Uncle Bill, and Aunty Jean burst in.

"I'm not going to do it, Mabel,"
Grandpa was saying. He looked really
grumpy and was shaking his head.

"I'm keeping these teeth forever."

They were the most disgusting pair of false teeth you've ever seen.

"They're so worn!" said Grandma.

"It would be much easier to chew with new ones," said Mom.

"I can chew just fine with these," said Grandpa.

"As long as he can drink his tea, Grandpa is happy," said Aunty Jean.

"Happy birthday, Grandpa," I said.

Grandpa grunted and gave me a pat on the shoulder.

"These teeth are comfortable, and I don't want new ones. They're in, and they're staying in," said Grandpa.

37

CHAPTER 4

Grandpa Loves Chocolate Crackles

Grandpa looked around at the party food. "This looks great! Did you make all this?" Grandpa asked me.

"Some of it," I said with a quick look at Mom. "I opened the jar of pickled onions for you."

"My favorites!" said Grandpa as he picked up the bowl. He started eating the onions as if they were popcorn. Old people have the strangest tastes!

"Dad!" said Mom. "The party doesn't start until the others get here."

"**My** party," said Grandpa with his mouth full of onions. "**My** food." He began looking around the table.

"Aha!" he said. "Chocolate crackles."

"Chocolate crackles?" said Mom. "I didn't make chocolate crackles."

I was feeling pretty proud of myself.
It was probably the first time I'd ever
done anything useful in the kitchen.

"I made them, Grandpa," I said,
holding up the plate for him. "They're
not set yet, so you'll have to hold
them carefully."

Grandpa put the now empty onion bowl down and rubbed his hands.

"After pickled onions," he said, "there's nothing I like better than chocolate crackles."

He scooped up two, one in each hand. Then he jammed them into his mouth, one right after the other.

He had a strange expression on his face. At first I thought it was because his false teeth weren't working. Then I realized that his teeth wouldn't make his eyes bulge.

There was a rumbling sound coming from him. It sounded like a really deep chuckle.

Suddenly Grandpa's cheeks puffed up, and white foam came out of his mouth.

"What's happening?" Aunty Jean screamed.

"He's foaming at the mouth!" said
Uncle Bill.

"His insides are coming out!" yelled
Grandma.

"What did you put in those chocolate crackles?" screeched Mom.

Grandpa's cheeks puffed and sank.
A great tide of foam poured out of his
mouth. With it came two pink and
yellow things.

Then I realized what they were—
Grandpa's teeth!

CHAPTER 5

Will Grandpa Be OK?

"Is this what you used?" Mom said, waving the empty box at me.

"Isn't that what you put in chocolate crackles?" I asked. "I've seen you put white stuff in."

"Powdered sugar! Powdered sugar, not baking soda!" Mom dropped the box and covered her face with her hands.

I was really worried. She seemed so upset. What had I done to Grandpa? Does baking soda hurt you?

Mom looked up. She wasn't crying at all. She was laughing! Laughing so much her mouth was wide open, and I could see all of her fillings.

"The baking soda reacted with the pickled onions," she said, laughing.

I suddenly remembered a science
experiment at school. Mix vinegar and
baking soda, and you get white foam.
It's how you make pretend volcanoes.

I looked at Grandpa. The stuff coming
out of his mouth was the same as the
stuff we made at school. Only we put
red coloring in ours so it looked more
like hot lava. Grandpa's foam just
looked like lots of toothpaste bubbles.

The difference was that his teeth had come out in these bubbles.

Grandma noticed that, too.

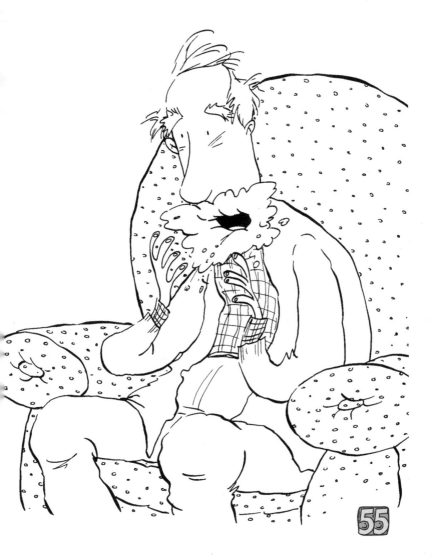

She moved faster than I'd ever seen her move. Darting forward, Grandma grabbed Grandpa's teeth.

"Gibembag," said Grandpa.

"No," Grandma patted her pocket. "They're out, and they stay out until you get new ones."

You can't argue with someone who's got your teeth! Especially if no one can understand you.

Grandpa sighed, spraying everyone with great gobs of white foam.

In the end, Grandpa had a great 80th
birthday. He sat on a chair in the
middle of the room eating mashed
birthday cake all afternoon.

He told me that there was one good thing about my mistake. The indigestion he'd had for three years was gone. It must have been the giant dose of baking soda.

Even though Grandpa ended up being happy about my mistake, Mom isn't taking any chances. She's signed me up for a cooking class. She says I need to learn the basics.

I just hope we don't have to eat the things we make!

GLOSSARY

 baking soda
a powder used in cooking
to help things rise

bulge
stick out

 **desperate**
having no hope

gritty
feels like bits of sand

indigestion
upset stomach

nibble
to eat little bits of

pantry
a closet where food is kept

waggled
moved with short, quick movements

Talking with the Author and Illustrator

Pam Harvey (author)

What is your favorite thing?
A silver bracelet that is made out of two spoons.

What do you like about yourself?
I like the way I smile a lot.

What is your favorite midnight snack?
Dried fruit, so I don't wake everyone.

Janine Dawson (illustrator)

What is your favorite thing?
Cracking up over something that the cats did (like when one springs straight up in the air!).

What do you like about yourself?
The fact that I love to draw.

What is your favorite midnight snack?
Toast and honey.

sundance™
A Haights Cross Communications ● Company

Copyright © 2002 Sundance/Newbridge Educational Publishing, LLC

Published by Sundance Publishing
P.O. Box 740, One Beeman Road, Northborough, MA 01532
800-343-8204

Copyright © text Pam Harvey
Copyright © illustrations Janine Dawson

First published 1999 as Sparklers by
Blake Education, Locked Bag 2022, Glebe 2037, Australia
Exclusive United States Distribution: Sundance Publishing

ISBN-13: 978-0-7608-8101-9
ISBN-10: 0-7608-8101-4

Printed in China